This book belongs to:

....

....

....

For Little Bear – F. H.
For William and Edward – S. H.

A BRUBAKER, FORD & FRIENDS BOOK,
an imprint of The Templar Company Limited

First published in the UK in hardback and softback in 2014 by Templar Publishing,
Deepdene Lodge, Deepdene Avenue, Dorking, Surrey, RH5 4AT, UK
www.templarco.co.uk

ISBN (hardback) 978-1-78370-041-7
ISBN (softback) 978-1-84877-156-7

Printed in China

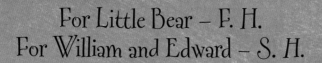

BRUBAKER, FORD & FRIENDS

AN IMPRINT OF THE TEMPLAR COMPANY LIMITED

George
and the
Dinosaur

written by
Felix Hayes

illustrated by
Sue Heap

This is George.

George likes digging.

So far he has found...

some gems,

a sword,

a pirate's wooden leg,

and,

to top off the hoard,

a **dinosaur**

egg.

George

loves

digging.

But,

when he cleans
his treasure,
he finds...

the gems
are stones, dirt
and dust.

The sword
is a spoon,
all covered
in rust.

The leg is a root,
cracked and dried.

But the egg's still an egg
with **something** inside.

George puts
the egg in the
cupboard under
the stairs.

George checks the egg every day.

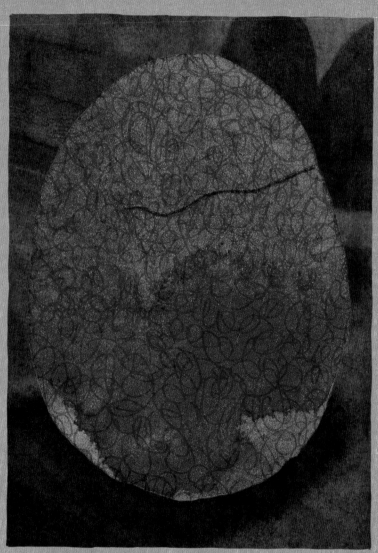

On the first day he hears a tap, tap, tap.

A few days later he spies a crack.

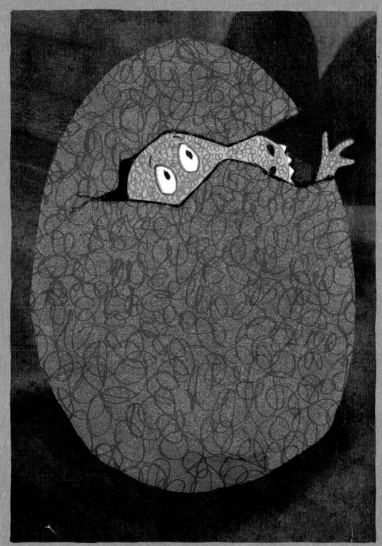

Then, when the egg starts to rumble and shake…

"Oops," thinks George. "Have I made a mistake?"

But after a week
he opens the door...

And there it is –

HIS DINOSAUR!

With fins down its back and lots of teeth,
it is green on top and yellow beneath.

With just one look,
George is sure
this is no ordinary
dinosaur.

It looks around.

"Mummy?"
it says.

"Er… yes?"
says George
and pats its head.

George thinks
his dinosaur is

perfect.

The dinosaur looks hungry,
so George gives it his lunch.

He gives it...

an apple, a sandwich,

some chopped-up carrot,

and a ginger biscuit
in the shape
of a parrot.

But his
dinosaur
still looks

hungry.

So George takes his dinosaur into the kitchen.

When he opens the fridge, on comes the light, and his dinosaur

eats...

mum
my
dinosaur
was
hungry!

ABC

Pizza

everything in sight:

the milk, the cheese,
some chocolate mousse –
all washed down
with pineapple juice.
It even eats mould
from a jar at the back.
But all of this food
is only a snack.

His dinosaur
still looks
hungry.

So George finds it some more things to eat.

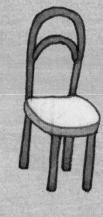

It eats all the plates
from the cupboard downstairs,
the towels from the bathroom,
the table and chairs.

It gobbles down books
and a tangerine,
the fridge, the TV
and the washing machine,

a tree from
the garden,
the paddling pool…

and Class 2's mouse on loan from the school.

(George never liked the mouse much so he doesn't mind.)

George thinks his dinosaur HAS
to be full by now.

But the dinosaur smiles a wicked grin,
and opens its mouth to stuff more in.
Mum's best dress, the lamp from the hall,
the dog, its lead, and its red squeaky ball.

Even Mum and Dad
are just a bite
for a
**greedy
dinosaur's**
appetite!

The dinosaur
scoops up George
and sets off into
town...

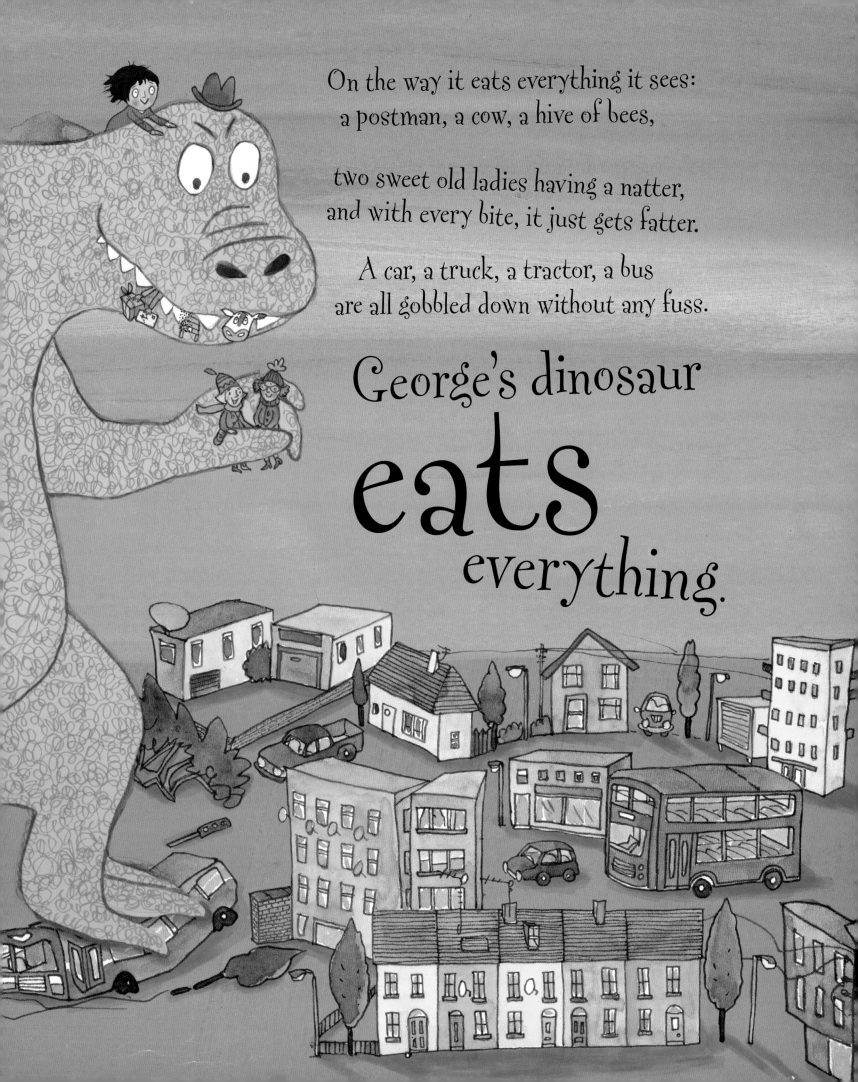

On the way it eats everything it sees:
a postman, a cow, a hive of bees,

two sweet old ladies having a natter,
and with every bite, it just gets fatter.

A car, a truck, a tractor, a bus
are all gobbled down without any fuss.

George's dinosaur
eats
everything.

And I mean **everything!**

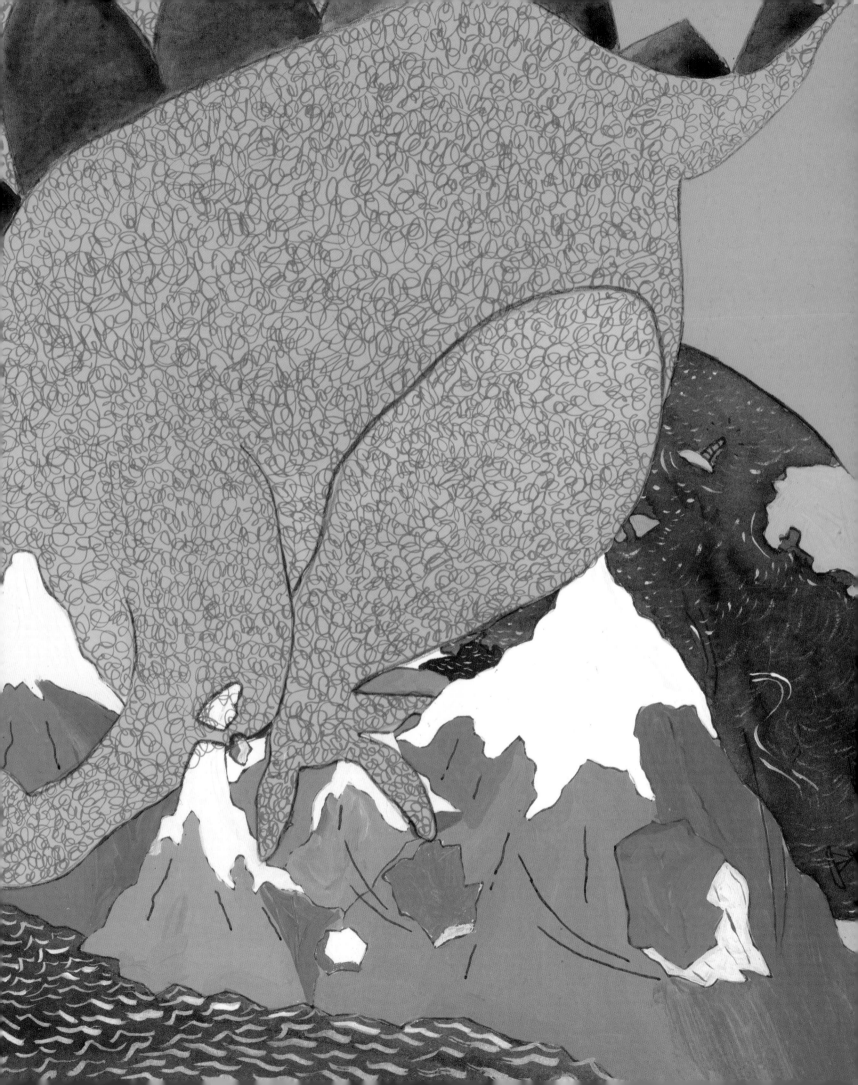

Finally, nothing is left...
Nothing at all.
Not a bean, not a mouse.
Nothing except...
George.

George looks at the dinosaur,
the dinosaur
looks at him,
opens
its
terrible jaws

and...

pops him in!

Then something starts to happen.
The dinosaur's tummy begins to bubble and squeak.
Its guts first gurgle and then they creak.
Its belly starts to rumble, and then to quake.

"Oops!"

it thinks, "I've made
a mistake!"

Its tummy swells
as it slobbers and slurps,
then the greedy dinosaur
finally…

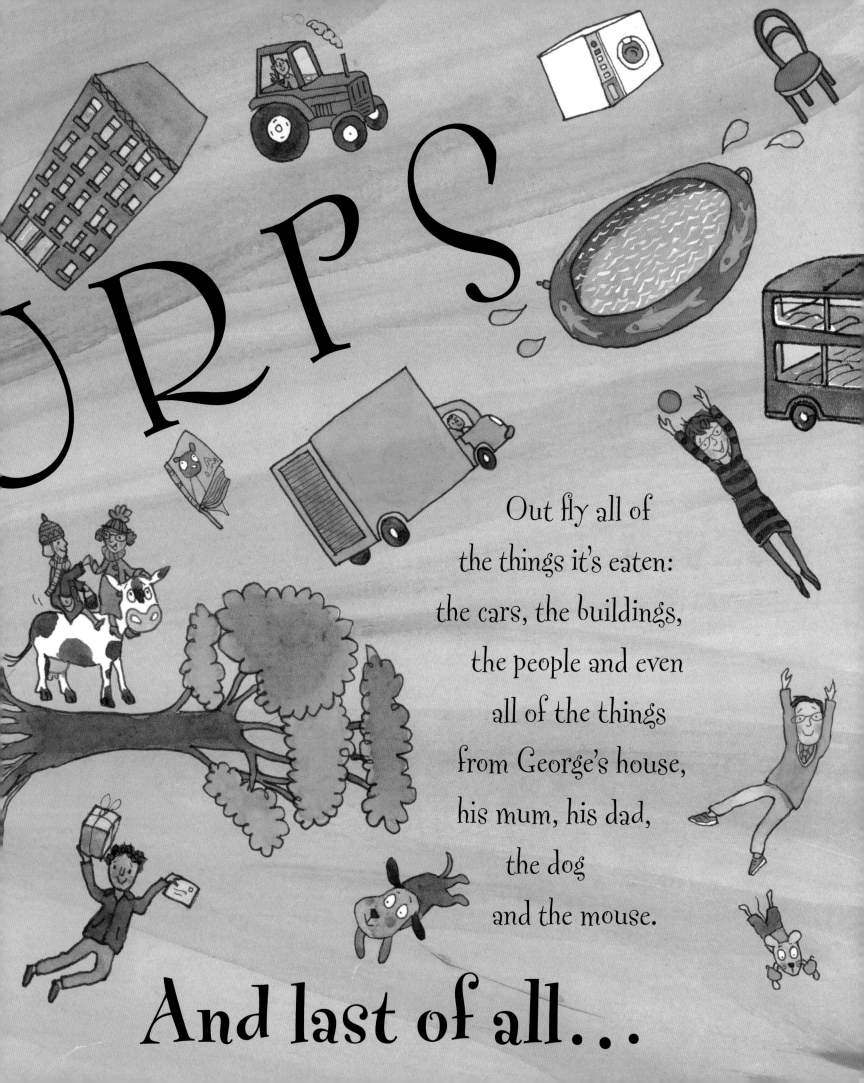

JRPS

Out fly all of
the things it's eaten:
the cars, the buildings,
the people and even
all of the things
from George's house,
his mum, his dad,
the dog
and the mouse.

And last of all...

... George!

"Well, that was fun!"
he says.

He dusts himself down and gets to his feet.

"Do we still need to find
you things to eat?"

The dinosaur looks sheepish
and shakes its head.

"Then pick up that spade
and let's **DIG** instead!"

I wonder what they will find next...